To:

From:

My Little One

A Mother's Lullaby

Written by Gerri Ann Wilt

Illustrated by Shannon Marie Sargent

For the love of my life for fifty years, my husband Tom. Thank you for your love and encouragement.
For my beautiful daughters, Sally, Susan, Shannon, Stacey, and Sarah. You were my inspiration to compose
and sing this lullaby over and over again.
I love you all.
G.A.W.

I would like to dedicate this book to my mom, Gerri, whose unwavering belief in my abilities has allowed me
this opportunity to be a part of something so dear to her heart; my husband, Sean, who is my strength, my
support, and my love, and my children, Brendon, Christopher, and Kailyn, who are my life.
S.M.S.

ISBN-13: 978-0-87839-299-5
Printed in the United States of America
Published by North Star Press of St. Cloud, Inc.
northstarpress.com   info@northstarpress.com

My Little One I saw you,
It was love at first sight.

I fed you.

I bathed you.

I put you to sleep.

This will not do!

I started to hum.

You stopped crying.

Go to sleep and dream awhile.
Greet the new day with a smile.

Little One
My Little One
Now the day is done.

Little One
My Little One
Now the day is done.

What a wondrous day we've had.
Full of joy for Mom and Dad.

Now it's time to go to bed.
Rest your sleepy little head.

Little One
My Little One
Now the day
is done.

Little One
My Little One
Now the day is
done.

Morning's coming close,
my dear.
Close your eyes
without a tear.

Soon the sun will shine,
and then
Playtime will be here
again!

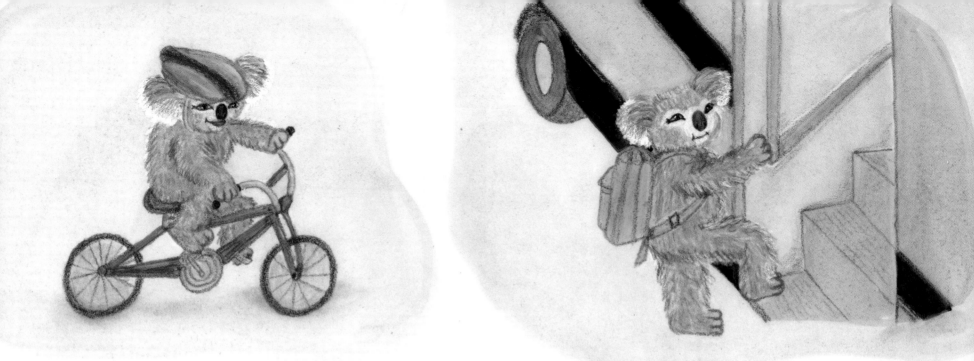

"My Little One" put you to sleep.

Now you sing it
to your little one.

Now I sing to
your little one.

"Sing 'Little One,' Grandma!"

Little One
My Little One
Now the day is done.

Little One
My Little One
Now the day is done.

My Little One

Gerri A. Wil